Dream Atlas
published for Scavel an Gow
by Giss'on Books
Halwinnick Cottage
Halwinnick Butts
Linkinhorne
Callington
Cornwall PL17 7NS

The writers of these stories assert the moral right to be identified as the authors in accordance with sections 77 and 78 of the UK Copyright, Designs and Patents Act 1988.

First published 2002

ISBN Number 0-9542150-1-X
Set in Perpetua 11.5/13.5
Printed by Printout Printing Service, Studios 1 & 2 Langarth, Threemilestone, Truro TR4 9AN

Dream Atlas

Scavel an Gow

Introduction

Scavel an Gow is a Cornish collective of writers united by a strong sense of place and a diversity of styles.

Scaval an Gow means 'Bench of gossip' in Cornish dialect, reflecting both the inspiration for the stories and the way we present them to the public.

In the last year we have been in receipt of a Regional Arts Lottery Grant from South West Arts. As well as publishing this book we have printed stories on paper bags to be handed out in shops in Newlyn and postcard stories for display on notice boards on Bodmin Moor. David Kemp has been commissioned to create a storytelling boat which sails into village halls, gardens, castles and quaysides for performances. Most recently we have been commissioned by The Eden Project to write stories from paintings by John Dyer of Mediterranean plants and fruits.

Dream Atlas has been produced in conjunction with a commission from BBC Radio 4. The stories were broadcast in September 2002, directed by Claire Grove.

Previous publications include: Shop of Stories and Homecomings (both with Kneehigh Theatre) and Kernow Bys Vyken (with the Hall for Cornwall).

All the illustrations in the book are original pen and ink drawings by Anthony Crosby, with the exception of the photograph accompanying Lydia Chicken which is reproduced by kind permission of Morrab Library.

November 2002

With Thanks

As with all endeavour many people and groups provide help on the way, we thank them all, in particular: Claire Grove, Martin Eddy, Morrab Library, John Harry and Kneehigh Theatre for starting us off, Steve Tanner and South West Arts.

Contents

Story illustrations
Anthony Crosby

Annamaria Murphy was a secret writer for many years. Then wrote a part for herself to avoid playing a dog. Since then has written for Kneehigh Theatre, Theatre Alibi, The Eden Project and Brainstorm Films amongst other things.

Simon Parker writes monologues, short stories, plays, poetry and songs. He was awarded the Henry Jenner Cup *(A Star On The Mizzen)*, Sybil Pomeroy Cup *(Charles Lee and the Newlyn School)*, Rosemergy Cup, and was short listed for the Daphne du Maurier Prize. Founder of The Charles Lee Society and Giss 'on Books, he is editor of *Living Cornwall* and *Scryfa*.

Paul Farmer, scriptwriter, playwright, and writer of short stories. He has written and directed films in both English and Kernewek. He is currently exploring Morocco for his latest project.

Amanda Harris is a writer and director of Kernow Education Arts Partnership which is dedicated to creating opportunities for teachers and artists to work together for mutual inspiration.

Pauline Sheppard, playwright and performer, has lived and worked in Cornwall since 1972. Her play *Dressing Granite* was nominated for the Meyer-Whitworth Award in 1997 and her most recent theatre work has been the adaptation of *The Ordinalia* for the community of St Just.

Stephen Hall, director of Golowan Festival and founder of *Tongue Pie*, story evenings in Penzance. He created the Penwith Community Archive in Oral History and was the Chair of Verbal Arts Cornwall. He is a storyteller, musician and songwriter.

Mercedes Kemp was born and grew up in Southern Spain but has lived in West Cornwall for thirty years. She is a writer of short stories and has also written for Kneehigh Theatre, both in Cornwall and Malta. She is currently working on a theatre project at The Eden Project based on the Mexican Day of the Dead. She is a senior lecturer in Education at Cornwall College, specialising in narrative approaches to practice.

Hidden Depths

by Stephen Hall

Daniel Gumb of Bodmin Moor was a king, the ruler of an unseen kingdom. His crown was ragged killas rock, his sceptre, sharp blackthorn. His great works are faint ciphers etched into corroding slate. Little is known. So much is lost.

He lived, breathed and bred nine children on the moor. I am one of the nine. I am a son of Daniel Gumb of Fawimore. I am the last to remember.

My father was born in the 'Great Tempest' of 1703, the 'Great Gale of violente winde' that sucked down the Eddystone Light and rolled up the wreck of ships and drowned sailors along the Cornish shores in burrs of timber, tar and bone.

At the very instant the storm blew one last raging dying blast, ripping slates, launders and rafters clean off the roof and the plaster ceiling above a soft plumpfy cradle, my father pitched, newborn wet and wailing, into this world. In the deep quiet that followed, still as a saucer of scalded milk, my swaddled baby father lay in his mother's flotsam dusty arms, gazing up at the firmament of stars with a contented smile, as wide as heaven. They say the tempest turned his perfect infant mind inside out and let his imagination fly.

As a child he thought in torrents, as a boy in cascades, as a man in waterfalls and rapids. Some say he was 'touched – mad as a ship's monkey', the highest fool in Cornwall, ever strange, respected and feared as only the truly mad, wise, or saints can be. No leadline could ever plumb the fathomless dreams of Daniel's hidden depths.

By day Father's trade was a stone-cutter, a conjurer with cold chisels and feathers. No church-goer or chapel neither, he was the last word and 'the' writer of the last word on gravestones for gentry and yeoman farmers from Temple to Lewannick – to the back of the back of beyond.

But at nights, under the drum of the wind, he honed the sharpness of his mind with mathematics and astronomy, wrestling with the riddles of infinities, prime numbers, circles, calculus, tangents and conics. He built our home at the 'birth of the world' – at the Cheesewring, on the high roof of the moor, where far-off tors and carns seem like a scattered fleet on the crests of russet waves. Our house was Father's observatory, bounded with carved slate slabs – thirteen for Euclid's thirteen books of the Elements, inscribed keys to the mathematical and logical heart of Father's life work – the algebraic and solid geometric map of his world. But there was more, for he was engaged on a mystic journey into the deeps and tides of the lower world, governed by the unruly waxey, waning moons above, sinister, still places where swallows sleep winter through – as snowflakes – thick as carp scales, drapse the moor.

It was to be the hazard of his life. Slate was the canvas that marked the compass and map of that adventure.

His obsession cast him adrift from all that is safe and sound, marooned him on an island of dreams inhabited by the sons of Bathomet, the Knights Templar – the poor knights of Christ at Temple, and the three heads. Cast him alone into the sacred geometric heart of Fawimore. Trapped in a mangrove of infinities and wonders, he came to understand the voice of the moor, the great pictures in the fields, the flight of birds, the customs of stars and the signals of things to come.

My father intended a map. To show how the inner, outer and lower worlds were all as one – a perfect guide to the holy geometry of the sinews, ways, rivers, blood and breath of the earth above and below. He would chart the perfect symmetry of the physical, mortal and immortal world – the spirit of the earth, a mercurial harmonious vital current. It would be a map of dreams.

Proof was everything and his quicksilver mind stretched as if the cables of his wit would break. A vision grew in my father like a spike on the prickly tree – to prove things so.

He took to straying from his work, days at a time. Nights alone at haunted Roche Hermitage or enchanted St Nectan's well – wandering – home wet-leaking, too tired to sleep. Mother was resigned. She knew the mester's nature when they churched. She never expected to be disappointed thereafter. Living on the roof of the world you get used to the touch of passing clouds.

So here I am, sat on the sedgy banks of Dozmary Pool just as I did sixty years ago, wondering why father had brought me there. We sat for a long time watching clouds, like windswept swans, slide over the sheeny waters.

He talked of King Arthur and the 'lady of the lake' with breasts – floury white as Tredethy eggs. How she rose up from the unimaginable depths beneath to take the king's sword – Excalibur, needle sharp as a humming bird's copper beak.

There was an older king too, long forgotten, with a bloodline of stories flowing still on the moor. This bronze-tressed king died, entombed with a charmed golden cup. It was said that any soul could win immortal life if only to sap dry that enchanted gilded basin.

He explained how Squire Robartes of Lanhydrock and his tenants were all robbed and betrayed by his steward. Tregeagle was so wicked that even the gates of hell shut tight fast in his face. His torment was an endless unforgiving destiny of impossible tasks – to free his soul. I thought on that poor cursed sinner, thin as a sixpence, setting to drain bottomless Dozmary, year in year out, with a limpet shell – leaking like rain through a sieve. I felt pity for him. I never said.

Father took up a flat shard of slate, and on that smooth stone page he etched Daniel Gumb, Fawimore, year, month, day and hour, laid out neat as writing by hand.

"Remember this day, John," he said, heaving that rocky slice as far as he was able into the heart of the dark syrupy treacle water. I remember how that stone flew like a dipping swift, skimming and skipping on the brackish glaze. Then it was gone. Then we went home.

Two years and many months on a stranger came to our door. Rarely visited by the closest we were wholly unprepared for so remote and so foreign a visitor, more olive than brown – curling blackamoor whiskers with a broad chain of gold at his neck. Intertwining black serpents and magic characters wound round his arms from shoulder to braceleted wrists along white-palmed hands to gem encircled fingers. He was holding the slate cast into Dozmary Pool.

My father turned the stone over and over gazing on the traced markings in disbelief. This was some Christmas game – mischievous roguery, sport for hobelteehoys. Daniel Gumb would not be fooled by an impostering painted play actor. But it was no play, no May mockery or Christmas game. Rejib Khan took my father's hand, leading his fingers across his dark face and mustachio. There was no paint, no daub, no arabic gum. "Who is the fool now, Daniel?" he said.

A strange story unfurled – how a spice ship, addled with crazed sick men, lay becalmed, drifting helpless for weeks on the sultry seas of the Indies. The joy of the sudden wind that took them to a fire scorched island and the chance finding of my father's slate in a red lava field, under the sulphur shroud of a volcano.

So it was that a man of the Western moors and another of the Eastern oceans became companions in the search for the symmetry in all things – to reveal the great design, defined by the footfall of angels.

Watching the sapphire sun slipping into tin red dusk and damask night, they walked the deck of the moor, under azimuth constellations drifting through hazy shoals of stars. They listened to the quiet music of the world above and below.

We children heard stories of great white birds that never sleep, fiery whirlwinds, icy whirlpools, flying singing fish, livid green ribbons and shimmering taffeta lights in Northern skies, Hi Brazil, Rozengain, fabulous Madagascar, Malacca and Muscovy, giants of Patagonia, monsters of Goa, gods and idols, lands of frost and fire, spices, musk and sweet beeswax, of a world of dreams painted out on glowing ochre boulders.

Caradon and Minions were wrapped in a chill dew mist on the morning our guest and friend left for the Falmouth Roads. At the parting of their ways, all farewells done, father pressed a slight string tied pouch into Rejib's hands. I did not hear what was said between them but as we made our way up the steep drenched track home, father turned to watch the sun melting the morning mist on Caradon. "Now I must wait," he said.

My father waited, as we children grew and outgrew the house 'at the birth of the world'. Waited as his daughters married off foreign and sons took up trades far from home. Waited, long after mother was laid to rest and quarry work started up on the Pound. Waited, as Minions grew from a desolation into a straggling menagerie of tinners, adventurers, masons, engine men and strangers.

The King of Fawimore watched as the flesh of his kingdom was overthrown under his very feet, granite bones blasted, churned, driven with inclines and shafts for the sake of a new monarch of the moor – King Copper.

When the stones of the Elements, symbols and runes – the maps of Daniel Gumb's world – were cracked by the quarryman's hammer, father withdrew into his own world. When no letter or word came from Rejib Khan he supposed that misfortune had taken his friend from him. Dark night fell in his heart. His perfect mind slipped from his grasp like crystal glass and shattered. He died in the spring – the first day azure African swifts skimmed and dipped over Dozmary.

Fawimore was swept by a new wind of greed. As if the riches ripped from its heart were not enough, men's eyes turned to easier plunder, the riches of burial mounds, barrows, cists, cairns and quoits. And because they were not 'of the moor' they cared nothing for the old ways. The clatter of engines, the din of hammers, bright lamplight, blinded inner eyes and deafened ears that had once feared the legends of kings and the 'poebel vean', the small people. Nothing is sacred.

The burrowers of this Cornish El Dorado spread over the moor like rabbits. Warrens grew around any lump in the ground that might hide treasure. I know of farmers who cracked cromlechs with powder, careened capstones, and finding nothing but 'old pots' full of pilth and ash, swore, cursed and scattered their own bloodline like corn for fowls. I know tinkers who paid pence for copper bracelets and gold necklaces that dressed princes. I know families that left forever.

At last the fever spread to the doorstep of the Pound. No more than a shout from the roof of the world, wagons gathered at the Hurlers stones. The talk and scandal was that the mound at Rillaton would be the next to fall to iron bar and black powder. Gentry and scholars gathered on the trampled scarred gorse portal of Rillaton. A flurry of rumour became a flood of news spreading beyond parish, town and country. The eyes of the world fell on the moor.

By order no black powder could be used and in recognition of the public interest a time was agreed for the 'great revealing', on the Monday next. A great assembly of neighbours, farmers, tinners, gentry and strangers gathered in the mire of that morning to watch the harnessing of twelve heavy horses, the raising of beams, windlass and chains. And I, John Gumb, the last son of the King of Fawimore, was amongst the small party chosen to break open the barrow.

This was no ordinary time. There were stories in the parish. There were signs.

On Sunday morning the little church at Temple had all of a sudden dropped, noiselessly, as soft as a falling feather, a fathom into the valley, so subtle and soft that sleeping moths fell on the heads of the congregation. In the churchyard ash branches moaned and creaked like aching limbs. Within the hour a great oak tree at Lewannick descended three fathoms into the ground taking with it a roost of quietly sleeping ravens in a flurry of leaves.

As the first sealing slab fell away the sudden sun struck into the ground's dark heart and there, perfect, pollen yellow on the peat floor was a cup, a breathtaking chalice. It was the same cup, remembered in the telling of a thousand generations, in the story told by my father, here, on the banks of Dozmary. It was the king's golden cup.

But there was a greater and richer treasure in Rillaton barrow, something too insignificant, everyday and ordinary to be noticed by antiquarians and scholars. I have it with me now on the banks of Dozmary Pool.

The knot is not difficult to untie and the contents of this slight pouch are worth little four – simple beads of amethyst, obsidian, faience and amber together with four precise rectangles of slate. On one side of each is an exact but unknown geometric figure. On the reverse of the first is written 'Daniel Gumb'. On the second 'Born in the great storm of 1703'. On the third 'The King of Fawimore'. On the fourth 'The Map Maker'.

My Name Is Lydia Chicken

By Annamaria Murphy

Oh I'm bound to leave you
Shallow oh Shallow Brown
Oh I'm bound to leave you
Shallow oh Shallow Brown.
Sell me for a dollar
Shallow oh Shallow Brown
Sell me for a dollar
Shallow oh Shallow Brown.

I'm lookin' straight at it. It's that photograph that was took. It says on it: 'The Bolitho Family, Trengwainton House 1850 with unknown Servant Girl.'

But that's me, that's me lookin' out. And my name is Lydia Chicken. That's who I am. It sure is. As sure as eggs is eggs. My father was the Chicken Man. As sure as eggs is eggs he was the Chicken Man. Makes sense to call a man after his work. How else should he be known? He had a another name but no one could say it. Not me, not the masters, not the others. He sang his song with a voice as deep as the mines: "Oh I'm bound to leave you, Shallow oh Shallow Brown." And I reply to him:

Sell me for a dollar
Shallow Oh Shallow Brown

I can't see him no longer, but I hear him down the long corridors, out in the yard, pluckin' them chickens, feathers stickin' to 'im, lookin' like a strange bird himself.

They go down them mines white and they come up black. Father said we'd be equal down there, no one could tell the difference, the only thing white would be the whites of our eyes.

My name is Lydia Chicken. It sure is. It sure as hell is. If you say your name loud enough people will know who you are.

Today I am dressed in white. I got a posy pinned on, Lily of the Valley, give to me by Rose who does the laundry. It smells lovely and I sure am glad of it near my nose. Sometimes the old ones smell. Father did say that when a person is near to the end you can smell it. He always knew.

I'm carrying the tea tray today. I never done that before. The cups is bone china. Rose says they're made from the bones of the old ones. I can't believe everything she says, but she sure was right about Ellen's belly gettin' bigger.

I'm walking down the corridor with the tea tray. The cups is shakin' like old teeth when they'm cold. My heart's beatin' like a flutterin' butterfly. I ain't never served the tea before. What if I spill it, burn the thighs of the old ones? They got see-through skin anyways, wouldn't take much to burn right through it. I seen the Mistress's blood once…same colour as mine!

"What you starin' at girl?" she said. "Haven't you ever seen blood before?"

No, I thought, not white people's blood. I didn't know it was the same colour.

Down the corridor the ancestors are starin' at me. "Bolithos goin' way back," says Rose. "That one there, John Bolitho Senior, is the one that first went out to, to Jammy-acre, or some such place, where your father and mother was bought from."

I tried one time to look for it on the Atlas that the Master has in his study, but the world didn't make no sense to me. Sometimes I dream of the fruits Father told me about, mangoes, flesh orange as sunset, chillis that sting your tongue an' wakes your body up right down to your toes. I ain't never tasted it, I only dreams of it. They only eats white food here, heavy on the belly, maybe it's white because it keeps their skins white? I asked Rose, but she didn't know. "One thing I do know though," she said, "Twasn't cream that made Ellen Gribble's belly grow!"

I'm nearly there now. The old ones are sitting outside waiting for their tea. They're all wearing black for mournin'. They been in mournin' so long, it won't ever be afternoon. I told this to Rose, and she said: "My Christ, Lydia, you made a joke!"

I'm there now. I'm some glad I got this Lily of the Valley pinned on. Old Grandma Bolitho smells strong today. They all got hair like wisps of smoke. It ain't got no spring in it, no life. Rose says mine's like a naughty child, won't stay in its place, springs up like heather underfoot. Well, who's this now, this young man, he's got one of them cameras. Rosemary says its all the rage now for the big families to have their pictures taken. I better stand out of the way.

"Lydia, Lydia Chicken, come here girl," says old Mr Bolitho, "You stand by Mrs Bolitho, girl."

I do it. My hands are tremblin' like the old ones. "Hold the tray," says the young man.

I do it. The cups shake like old bones dancing. "What's wrong with you Lydia?" says young Mrs Bolitho, 'cept well she ain't that young, but younger than the old ones, she ain't quite got the smell of death yet.

And then, flash! He takes one of them pictures. With me in it too.

I tell Rose they had me in the picture. She can't believe it. "They want to show how fancy they are I 'spect, show they got a coloured girl servin' their tea."

She's probably right, she usually is.

Oh Father, where are you? You could not smell it on yourself could you? That near-the-end smell. The chickens still run when they hear boots. They think it's you comin' for them, but it's only me come to feed them. Sometimes I think I hear you singing, amongst the flying feathers.

Oh I'm bound to leave you
Shallow oh Shallow Brown

*

I John Bolitho never wanted no photograph taken, but as usual the women had their way. I don't know what's wrong with a painting, I said, it's been good enough for all the other Bolithos before us. But they wouldn't have it. I warned them. "Photograph idn't so flatterin'," I said, and I was right. You can tell I didn't want it done by the look on my face, an' they insist on showing it to every bugger who comes a-calling. They made Lydia Chicken stand in it too. Poor child was shakin' like a leaf.

I remember the day she was born, she lost her mother by the birth, we lost a good servant, and Jacob Chicken lost his wife. Well, I don't know that they was properly married. I brought 'em back from Jamaica. People say I'm a hard hearted bastard the way I work our Cornish lads down the Pilchard Works, but I'm not so hard hearted I would separate a man and his wife like some of the Bristol men did.

And, when he lost Sarah, his wife, his mate, whatever you like to call the arrangement, I took him off the pilchards and put him in charge of the chickens. I sometimes listened to his singing, and my famous granite heart would crack at the sound of it. I know beauty when I hear it. I shall not be remembered for my soft heart though, it will not be on my grave stone, 'John Bolitho. Remembered for his soft heart and fair ways in business. Rest In Peace.' Ha!

It does not matter now. Now that we are flat and still, our old and wrinkled faces in a permanent grimace. I warned those women, I said: "You'll be better off with a picture painted, you can't pick up a great heavy picture and fondle it about, there's no respect for something you can pass around from person to person, a photograph is too bloody flimsy." But they wouldn't listen.

"I wished we'd had one done of our son," said Emelia, my dear wife, "but you wouldn't have it would you, and his portrait is only half done."

I never seen her angry before. That's when she threw down one of her favourite china cups and cut her finger. Lydia stared at the blood like she'd never seen it before. A strange child that one. Sometimes she speaks like her father and sometimes like a true Cornish maid.

I caught her once scrutinising my old Atlas, runnin' her fingers across the flat countries of the world. Maybe her hands were searching for home, though she never has been there, maybe she could feel the rivers and the valleys and see them in her mind's eye. Maybe she dreams her mother's dreams. I don't know, I never had the notion to ask her. Sometimes I have dreamt at night that I am eating the soft flesh of mango and woken up dribbling on the pillow.

When Lydia Chicken was born, I peeped in to have a look. My granite heart cracked a little more at the sight. I had not been allowed in to see my own son born, to see what sort of a man he would make.

I can't abide all these visitors we have now, traipsin' through the house uninvited, breathin' on all my kin, touchin' all my furniture with their sticky fingers, even though it says clearly not too.

They tut-tut about my plantations…but they still don't mind a bit of sugar in their tea do they?

Things haven't changed that much.

*

Me tongue can't get around me own name now, it forgotten the shape of the sounds of me own mother-given name, me own father-given name. Me tongue need juice to say me name, mango juice, sweet dark rum. The words in this place are hard like the stone. After a while me throat dries out and I can't say me own name no more, so I settle for Jacob Chicken. I say to Lydia: "Lydia girl, shout your name out so as you know who you are, if you shout loud enough girl, they hear it across the ages."

We practise sometimes, when we chase them chickens. The squawkin' drowns out us shoutin' our names. Sometimes we laugh amongst the feathers. The girl Rose come one time and we all three shout our names.

You see, we got no gallery of ancestors hanging on the walls so we must shout loud.

Lydia born free, but where she got to go? Her hands run free over Mr Bolitho's Atlas. Them chickens is more free. We walk down the street in Penzance town an' every head turn, and I tell you, it ain't because we was wearin' no fancy hats!

Down in Mr Bolitho's Pilchard Works it sure was dark. First day I was there, men asked whether I was the same colour all over. Well I showed 'em. I stood naked as a fish amongst them barrels. And they never asked me no more. "You're the same man as us," they said.

I don't know about that.

The fish oil smelt the same on my hands as it did on theirs. Them chickens smell no better. I love them chickens. They dream of flight like I dream of the big Jamaican sun.

Now, I don't smell of nothin'.

I watch my Lydia wobblin' down the hall of ancestors, they lookin' at her as if they know better, she carryin' a tray of tea an' I can hear her heart beatin' like rumblin' ground. She wearin' a white dress an' flowers at her breast. I'm glad for that. Old Grandma Bolitho don't smell too good, an' it's one thing I don't miss. Lydia's hair tryin' its best to break free. What they want her for I don't know. There was some things I never did tell her. I never did tell her why the girl Ellen's belly swelled out. It should be a mother who tells those things. It wasn't me, oh no, not Jacob Chicken, an' I can't tell who it was. Them ancestors know though, lookin' down with their beady painted eyes, they sure do know.

Mrs Bolitho, she don't know, an' young Mrs Bolitho she don't know either.

But I know one who does know, as sure as eggs is eggs. An' of course the girl Ellen, she knows. She sure as hell does. An' when the child comes out, that Ellen will shout out that name, and then, the chickens will fly. The walls will shake. Be careful my girl Lydia Chicken, there are things I should have told you. About men.

*

I'm comin' back down the corridor, hurryin' past them long ago Bolithos. But what's this? It's a great crowd of them visitors, they'm in a big flock, starin' at the paintings, touchin' the furniture. I better hide in here… the Masters' study…no…they're comin' in here…

I'm hidin' behind the big, crimson curtain, heavy as sleep and the dust floats up like dreaming.

Look, look at that, they're lookin' at the photograph, the one with me holdin' the tray with my fingers tremblin'.

"Thats me," I say. But no one hears.

They leave the Master's study. I come out from behind the curtain. A child turns round.

"Look Mummy," she says. "There's the lady from the photograph."

The mother looks.

"There is no lady sweetheart," she says.

No one's called me a lady before.

I shout my name loud.

"I am Lydia Chicken, I sure as hell am, I am Lydia Chicken!"

They all leave, the visitors.

"Lydia," I shout after them, "Lydia Chicken!" The girl and her mama buy tea from a counter. They go to sit where I stood with the old ones. I watch that little girl.

"Lydia," she says to herself, "Lydia Chicken."

Someone has heard my name.

Wild Oats

by Simon Parker

"Porridge, love?" Frank called to his sleepy son. "I've made plenty." He always made plenty. He always made the same amount in fact. One mug of pinhead oats, three mugs of water and a good pinch of salt. Frank was a porridge eater – and champion of its various qualities and delights – by circumstance, not by birth. He hadn't always made porridge. But since marrying Maire he had embraced those aspects of her Scottish culture he took a fancy to. Porridge, square sausage and single malts were eagerly welcomed into his life. Jimmy Shand, midges and mutton pies he might never get used to.

Frank had always lived in the bustling, scruffy fishing port on the toe of Cornwall. It was his home all right, but that didn't stop him from yearning to turn his back on it for a bit and to see just a little of the world.

Maire had sailed into his life on a mist-heavy sea, and he immediately fell for her mane of jet hair as she climbed the granite steps of the harbour when the boat she was helping to crew put into port for repairs en route from the Clyde to the Med. She never completed that journey, choosing instead to wave off the rest of her shipmates from the pier, her other hand firmly clutching Frank's calloused fist.

"Porridge?" he called again.

Laurence shuffled in, half dressed, half asleep and still half drunk from the night before.

"Porridge?" his father repeated.

"Is that all you've got my man?" said Laurence, feigning the accent of an upper class English gent. "How's a chap expected to enjoy a good day's shooting with just a bit of gruel in his gullet? Where are the devilled kidneys, you scoundrel?"

Father and son laughed, embracing gently and comfortably. "Porridge it is then," said Laurence, settling down to read the jobs page of the local newspaper.

This ritual, or one very similar, was acted out nearly every morning; for Frank and Laurence it was as much a part of waking as yawning. Maire had become oblivious to their antics, quietly drinking her tea and listening to the radio news as her two 'boys' sniggered at their own performances, which became more bizarre and theatrical by the day. Every morning Maire's contribution to the drama was to suddenly transform from a silent, calm and near-motionless creature into a dervish, jumping up, crying something about the time, rummaging about in a desperate search for keys, purse, coat, shoes, kissing Frank and Laurence, and flying out of the front door.

Maire worked in a bookshop. She was assistant manager, though the title meant little. But she enjoyed her work, meeting other enthusiastic bookworms, avid children, and elderly self-educated gentlemen. Finding and ordering a title to replace a lost and cherished memory from someone's childhood was a regular request, and her particular joy. Every hour spent poring over catalogues, telephoning publishers and speaking to antiquarian dealers – and they were usually as antiquarian as their wares – was worth it just to see a customer's face as he or she was transported back decades to a lost childhood day or a time when their lives were simpler, less cluttered.

Frank had worked for years as a harbour odd-job man. His was the lot of many Cornish men with few qualifications but nevertheless a fierce determination to resist the well-trodden route of so many of their peers, forced to leave the land of their birth to find employment up the line. So he picked daffodils and broccoli in the season, mended stonework, collected port rents, helped in the café and generally kept the quayside tidy and ticking. Poorly educated and poorly paid, he was treated as an ignorant dogsbody by some of the wealthy sailors who now used the quay and whose presence was beginning to become almost as important to the port as the long-liners, crabbers and trawlermen whose forebears had built the harbour.

But despite a lack of prospects, Frank always had his dream. He'd had the same consuming ambition for almost as long as he could remember. He'd had it in fact since his own father had given him a copy of Laurie Lee's *As I Walked Out One Midsummer Morning* when he was ten years old. His father said he'd found it floating – actually floating – in the harbour amongst a raft of flotsam.

"The darnest thing," his father had said, as he handed it to Frank. "The darnest thing." And he shook his head, smiling in a kind of wonder and disbelief.

Frank read it over and over until the pages became frayed and the cover had to be repaired with Sellotape. And as he read it, his dream was born: to one day save enough money to travel to a distant port and there wander freely and poetically on foreign soil.

But it wasn't to be. Frank had his dream roughly snatched from him one squally July afternoon when an untidy Force 8 was making conditions in the bay difficult for sailors and fishermen alike. He was busy making fast everything along the south pier, tying down tarpaulins and securing mooring ropes, when a rich but inexperienced 'yacht yob' with "money aplenty but shit for brains" as Frank put it, lost control of his rig and let the boat's boom swing wide of the quayside. All its weight and force, boosted by a 60mph gust, smashed Frank's legs against a granite mooring post.

Of course, he could have been killed. That's what the yachtsman's smart lawyer argued, as if it were some consolation to a man who for a while thought he'd never walk the length of the quay again, let alone wander freely and poetically on foreign soil.

The compensation itself seemed quite fair at the time. But Frank was two years without work and they couldn't go another winter without replacing the cottage's old corrugated iron roof. In no time those precious few thousand pounds were gobbled up. And with it Frank's dream of seeing the world.

Then there were Laurence's violin lessons, they had to be paid for – Frank wouldn't have it any other way. Laurence didn't actually want violin lessons, but Frank was insistent. It was simply a case of "my son's going to have all the things I never could". Maire thought it unwise to persist with the argument that even though Frank felt deprived as a child because his parents were too poor to be able to afford music lessons, Laurence would feel similarly aggrieved, or even bothered. As it turned out, Laurence, to the silent disappointment of Frank, never took to the instrument. Even he had to admit – to himself at least – that there was very little one could describe honestly as musical in the scrapings Laurence made as he dutifully undertook his nightly practice. Frank didn't protest when these sessions began to get shorter and shorter until the forlorn little fiddle – and with it another of Frank's dreams – was left to gather dust on a shelf in the parlour while Laurence went off and practised his tail-flips and fakeys with the other skateboarders.

A couple of summers drifted by and before Frank realised what was happening, Laurence was no longer his little boy. He was a year out of school, and despite reasonable exam results, had no job – and with unemployment running at nearly sixty per cent of the male population in the area, little hope of one.

Frank knew Laurence was at that age when anything seemed possible and life stretched out before him like a long thin road, edged with trees in blossom, bathed in sunshine, full of promise. Frank could remember feeling like that when he was seventeen. There was no rush to get stuck into anything. Just let it happen. Laurence wasn't idle; he'd surf and swim and cycle. Sometimes he'd spend a whole day dangling a couple of hooks off the end of the South Pier, bringing home enough mackerel and pollock to give everyone in the terrace a good tea, and on warm summer nights, he and a few friends might light a fire in the dunes and just talk about nothing much until dawn.

Frank knew that carefree feeling, and saw so much of himself in the boy. Sometimes he'd sit and watch him when he knew Laurence was oblivious to his presence. He'd watch him lovingly wax his surfboard as the sun lit up his hair just before it slipped into the ocean. And at those moments he knew for sure that he loved him like no father had ever loved a son before.

It was for that reason that he set about plotting Laurence's future, a future full of adventure, of dreams fulfilled.

Where was that old copy of *As I Walked Out…?* Those tales of little Lolly Lee, who'd strolled away from his home and family with hardly a backward glance and found love and romance and poetry in Spain, had captivated Frank since he was a boy. He asked Maire to get him a new copy. She knew he kept the one his father had given him by the bedside, knew how important it was to him, knew in her heart that this fresh copy must be for Laurence. Knew he must be dreaming again.

The first morning after it arrived Frank rose early. Into the pot, as usual, went one mug of pinhead oats, three mugs of water and a good pinch of salt. Then, as the familiar brew began to bubble, Frank sprinkled in Page One of Laurie Lee's epic tale, which he had carefully chopped into fine dust with his best gutting knife.

"Porridge, love?" he called, and his son responded in the usual way before sitting down to his steaming bowl. On that first morning, Laurence unknowingly ingested *'the stooping figure of my mother, waist-deep in the grass and caught there like a sheep's wool'* and was quite unaware of the potency of each

spoon as its contents slipped down between mouthfuls of sweet tea. On Day
Two Laurence's intestines were *'affronted by freedom'* and on Day Three they
met *'an old hag with a tooth like a tin-opener'*. On Day Four he was serenaded
with *'tunes of sober zest'* and *'rewarded with silver'* while on Day Five *'a fluid
young girl of sixteen hugged him steadily throughout one long hot day with only a
gymslip on her sea-wet body'*.

And so it went on. Each breakfast-time Laurie took Laurence on a
journey of discovery from Zamora to Valladolid, Segovia to Madrid, Toledo to
Malaga – and all to the impassioned accompaniment of a gypsy fiddle. Frank,
meanwhile, waited and hoped for any small sign that his son was
experiencing an awakening, some portent that a wanderlust was being
kindled from within.

And sure enough, one February morning – when Laurie had been *'in
Manolo's Bar muttering about civil war'*– Laurence told his father, quite casually,
that "a few of us are thinking 'bout buying a round-the-world ticket, do a bit
of surfing and stuff, there's too many local girls whispering 'bout marrying
and settling down". Frank smiled gently. Inside he was dancing.

"Home's not going nowhere, son," he told him. "It'll all still be here
when you get back."

After a summer saving every last penny earned slogging in hotel
kitchens at all hours, pulling potatoes, and taking holidaymakers on tours
round the bay, Laurence packed a single bag, strapped his surfboard on his
back, and was gone.

That night Frank read to Maire: *'She stood old and bent at the top of
the bank, silently watching me go, one gnarled red hand raised in farewell and blessing,
not questioning why I went.'*

They both held each other and wept. Happy for him, aware that he
had to go, but brimming with the anxiety felt by all parents.

*

After almost thirty years of 'bumming around the world' as he put
it, Laurence finally wandered home for good. Frank was long dead. But he'd
had one last dream. It concerned the letters Laurence had sent him each
week without fail from the places he visited – New Zealand, South Africa,
Cambodia, Guatemala and, of course, Galicia, where Laurie Lee first landed

and where the Atlantic breakers pound the northern Spanish coast in such a way as to create the most perfectly formed waves Laurence had ever surfed. Frank's dying wish was that Laurence's letters should be cremated with him and that the ashes were scattered to the four winds when the first Force 10 blew into the bay after his funeral service. "You see me travel then, boy," he'd said.

*

Laurence eventually took over the running of the bookshop which his mother had bought some years earlier. In old age, on winter days when no one came to buy, he liked nothing more than to sit by the paraffin stove in the back of the store room and to turn the pages of a novel set in a foreign land. He read avidly, for the first time in his life. Everything from Hemingway to Yevtushenko, Rushdie to Rulfo. He liked most writers...though strangely enough, Laurence found he never could quite stomach Laurie Lee.

The Love Of The Hermit For The Fisher Woman

by Mercedes Kemp

Nobody would have guessed that the night when all of the boats on the village put out to sea to witness the passing of the great ocean liner would also mark the beginning of a great love story. A love story of epic proportions that would plumb depths of despair as deep as the Marianas trench and soar to heights of elation only previously reached by the loftiest of migratory flocks.

The moon was already high when the great vessel appeared on the horizon, the hoarse sound of its siren shattering the night. A flotilla of rafts and boats of all sizes grouped in a semicircle and let off a fusillade of rockets and a blossoming of flares that hung in the black sky like God's lightbulbs. As the great looming mass of the transatlantic grew ever closer, crowned with its Babylon of lights and dance music, the villagers in their tubs, skiffs, trawlers and pilot boats cheered and fired fresh volleys of rockets and flares.

Later, some would say that it was the combination of the moon, the flares and the twinkling lights festooning the bridge that allowed him to see her; that as a seafarer and navigator he had unusually keen eyes. But it is hard to explain how the captain of the great liner, standing high on the bridge of his mighty ship, could have really seen the fisher woman in her tiny boat, how he could have seen her so clearly that he later said that it was the fierceness in her eyes that had robbed him of his will, her eyes that, he said, looked so like the eyes painted on the prow of her fishing boat.

He was too honourable a man to abandon the ship he commanded, and he completed what would be his final professional journey relying heavily on his training and his experience, as his will had been captured in the nets of the fisher woman.

His mates were astounded at first, then furious. "You are going to leave all this for some scraggy woman in a shit fishing village on some far corner of that stinking sea! A future of greasy sardines and slimy octopus! You were born to navigate the mighty oceans, not to chase sprats in a pond with a rowing boat."

He didn't even hear them; the needle on his compass was fixed. Leaving behind his gold braided coat and his captain's hat, but taking his brass telescope to look out for his beloved's return from daily toil and his mariner's pipe which would help him pass the hours while he waited, he set off on his journey. In his mind he was already safe in the fisher woman's arms. In his mind they had a present, a past and a future, endlessly loving on the shores of the sea of love, love wavelets lapping at their feet, tides of love sweeping over them, love storms raging with electric love.

But it was not to be. He arrived at the fishing village on a rare grey morning, the sky as leaden as the sea. She was pulling her boat on to the beach, looking bedraggled and damp. He ran towards her. She fixed him with her gorgon eyes, turned on her heels and stomped away. He thought he would die. His heart turned into a mourning albatross in his chest, its great dark wings flapping in an agony of despair. He felt like the shipwrecked sailor who, when setting eyes on the ghastliness of the desert island where the tempest has tossed him, wishes only to be swallowed up and drowned.

Shipwrecked as he was, he became a hermit. He made his cell at the far end of the beach, an upturned boat draped with old nets and a ballast of jetsam, in case of high winds. He had an oil drum where he sat every day with his telescope, looking out for the beloved, hoping beyond hope. The villagers ignored him, taking him for an anchorite seeking solitude and grateful that at least he had chosen the path of saintliness on his own two feet and could therefore feed himself, unlike the stilites of old who would perch themselves like old cormorants atop thin tall columns on the beach and expect to be fed by the villagers, lowering their little baskets on a rope three times a day like clockwork for breakfast, lunch and dinner.

For a while the hermit's old sea companions would call when passing by, bringing him copies of The Times and bottles of contraband brandy. In time, as he remained uncommunicative, they stopped coming. The months and years went by and his hair and beard grew long. His love for the fisher woman did not abate. As she would not come anywhere near him, he sought ways to communicate his love from afar. He raked the sand on the beach into fantastic swirling shapes that echoed the mystery of wave patterns. He shaped whales and dolphins out of damp sand and, once, a fabulous mermaid with seaweed hair, limpet eyes and a cowrie shell placed where her womanhood turned fish. The fisher woman landed her boat a little closer to the hermit's cell. He constructed a little forest of windvanes topped by constellations of starfish, flights of seagull feathers, shoals of fish skeletons. The fisher woman drew ever closer. One particularly warm night she slept on the beach. He could get close enough to see the salt putting a bloom on her skin. He liked the way her sleeping eyelids trembled as if holding tiny fish frantically swimming to and fro.

The next day, at dusk, she brought her boat into the beach. She bunched her skirts between her legs and sat on the still warm sand, expectant.

The hermit came out of his cell and began to dance. Holding indexes and thumbs together, he made his fingers into twin eye-shapes, fish-shapes undulating in the inky night air; she watched following the waving of his fingers with her fishy eyes. The hermit's head snaked, he clapped his hands and spread his arms out, rushing forwards like the fishing seabird, then stopped as if hitting the hard surface of the water, head poised sideways. His fingers snapped and he swayed and twirled again and again to the music of the waves.

The fisher woman looked at him and spoke for the first time. "If you can dance like that for me every night I will consider setting up my own shack at this end of the beach. Besides, I quite like a man who can make better use of a fishbone than using it for a toothpick."

Years have gone by, but sailors still speak of a remote stretch on the far shores of the oldest sea where the beaches grow fabulous forests of intricate sea treasure and, at dusk, a man can be seen dancing slow amorous dances to a fish-eyed fisher woman. They say that sometimes the sight of this beach makes them wish to abandon their mighty vessels, their gold braided coats and their seafaring ways, but in their hearts they know that they are really lesser men than their old companion, the hermit. So, with a blast of their sirens, they move on.

Terra Nova

by Paul Farmer

Edgar did not like artists and he wanted to go to bed. Instead he found himself in the noisy bar of the Artists Colony Club in Penzance drinking beer he didn't want, with a man he didn't like.

Edgar had resprayed the Mazda MX5 of Adrian Andrews, the Ludgvan Lothario, and now he wanted to be paid. Andrews was stringing this out. He was as demanding a customer as he was a careless driver, and the job had been long. Now Andrews was entertaining the "artists" within earshot in the role of "Careless Fop Debtor" with Edgar cast as "Philistine Person of Porlock". Adrian Andrews came to the Artists Colony Club only to enact his nightly pantomime of seduction. His art involved priming with large drinks and washing with a bucket load of bull. Andrews' ageing partners were in equal parts surprised and grateful.

Edgar knew little about art, and cared less. Ignoring Andrews' pretentious sallies, he stared at a corner of the ceiling and wished himself anywhere else.

"What are you working on?" Edgar turned to find himself addressed by a striking woman with long red hair, dressed in green clothes that matched her eyes. What was he working on? It seemed an odd question. "I start on a Nova in the morning," he replied. It was an uninspiring prospect, but the Vauxhall Nova was a car designed to reassure rather than to inspire.

Her full mouth fell open. "Nova? But that's my name!" she said. He hoped he would feel so affirmed if Vauxhall announced the launch of the Edgar GTi. Then her hand was on his chest, her face very close. "I hope you plan a montage in green and red?"

Edgar recalled that beige had been mentioned, but he enjoyed the woman's — Nova's — touch and agreed. "What do you work in?" asked Nova. She touched his cheek. "Acrylic?"

He caught sight of himself in a mirror behind the bar. Bugger, he thought. In his anxiety to get paid he had forgotten his nightly appointment with the Swarfega. Nova had mistaken the paint staining his skin and clothes for the stigmata of the artist. "Cellulose," he admitted. "Fascinating!" breathed Nova, "Brush or knife?"

"A compressor mainly," said Edgar. "And quite a lot of newspaper."

"That is so *interesting*!" she said. "Where do you work?" Edgar described at length the location of his back street shed. The geography of Penzance was a mystery to her. "Darling, I will come," said Nova, "I love to visit the artist in his studio. Au revoir!" She kissed him, lightly, but on the mouth.

As he watched her leave the room, Edgar felt a bundle of banknotes slipped into his hand. "I say!" purred Adrian Andrews, "Bravo!"

Edgar was sitting on the kerb smoking a rollup when Nova made her visit. She floated down the middle of the street, a shawl thrown round her shoulders, looking like the love interest out of Braveheart. She kissed him. "Where is your work?" she said. "Where is Nova?"

Inside the shed he showed her the car. Her face fell. "I know," said Edgar. "I'm sorry." "Quite," she said. "You promised me a montage of red and green and this work is – grey!"

"It's not finished," said Edgar, "That's just the primer."

"You must excuse me," said Nova, "I know nothing of this medium."

"Its not exactly a medium," said Edgar, "It's more of a – car."

"Edgar, you are the artist. To you it might say 'car'. But to me it says 'metal'. To me it says... 'Hard'." She thrust Edgar backwards across the bonnet of the Nova and did things to him that added a new set of shock absorbers to the cost of the repairs.

Not that the bill would ever be paid.

Alone again late that night, Edgar surveyed the Vauxhall Nova.

It was now a montage of dark red and green.

How would he explain this to Fungus Rowe? Fungus was a beige man. He definitely wasn't the montage type.

But luck it seemed had fallen in love with Edgar as suddenly he had fallen in love with the redheaded woman. Fungus, roaming the internet, had discovered a budget holiday site and come over spontaneously Balearic. He would not be back for a fortnight. It was in these days that Edgar too found himself in a new land. A new geography came to overlay the streets of his town, a new landscape of emotion and magic, significance, new possibilities of joy and pain. The new map was marked "Terra Nova".

Cornwall was Nova's "strange land". She had arrived in flight to the west from some event or situation upcountry that she would not talk about.

Trauma for her found release in mystery, and he, Cornish to the core, was its embodiment, with all the possibilities of exploration that come with the flesh. Their love was rooted in disorientation and misunderstanding, a gulf that took his breath away in a sort of romantic vertigo. He tried not to be frightened.

Nova moved into his house, though she would disappear for whole days and even whole nights. It disturbed Edgar that he didn't feel inclined to ask where she had been. He remembered how he and his ex-wife had torn each other apart because they cared so much, or at least felt they should. Nova was older than his thirty-two years, but she seemed to have beauty locked into her bones. Only when tired did her face dissolve into the knobbly and shiny facets that were the work of age in others and this made her seem ordinary and warmer.

For although they now lived only feet apart, from the moment they awoke they seemed to inhabit different planets. She would insist on breakfast coffee, though the thought made him gag. One morning she returned to bed with a bottle of white wine. She was distant then, thinking of something or someone far away. He drank strong tea, which she said reminded her of wet dogs, preferring the scented and flowery varieties bought from the kind of Causewayhead shop he was too embarrassed to enter.

She filled his house, and particularly his bathroom, with hennaed, scented, hessian mysteries that filled the small spaces left by his own heaps of tools, CDs and feral paperwork. Altogether the mess was formidable and Nova would wave a languorous cigarette at it, as if to say, "Well, what would you?" But she did so lying long and pale on his bed, and that was what mattered.

As time passed Nova was coyly allowing herself to become aware of the true nature of Edgar's activities in the shed. The misunderstanding had almost become a joke. Edgar had enjoyed the rewards of being an artist, but he looked forward to the day Nova acknowledged that she was in love with a car sprayer and their two planets could at least orbit the same star. Then he could respray Fungus's car before he returned and they could get on with their lives free of misunderstandings, at least until they invented some new ones.

One day there was a knock at the door. Edgar opened it to find two men on the doorstep. One was small and scented and dressed in a crimson suit. The other was large, bald and moustached, and dressed in pale blue. They thrust past Edgar then paused in the living room, stunned in the face of so much stuff. The small crimson one snatched up Nova's necklace, which she had left hanging from the doorknob. "Ersss!" he said triumphantly to his companion in a deep foreign voice that belied the slightness of his frame. Nova appeared from the kitchen. "Edgar, have you seen my...?" At the sight of the intruders she stopped in confusion. "Bernard!" she said to the crimson man. After the smallest pause she turned to Edgar decisively and clapped her hands like Lady Bountiful doing good among the poor and needy. "You have some work outside," she snapped. "Ersss," said the little crimson man in confirmation. The large pale blue man looked meaningfully at the door.

Alone in the shed Edgar sat on the bonnet of Fungus's collage-car for some time, listening for sounds from the house. Nova hadn't seemed frightened by the two men, more embarrassed. By him. This brought heat to his cheeks and sent him hurrying outside. Bernard and his friend were leaving, laughing with Nova in a way that made it clear that these aliens were from her own, distant, planet. They turned to look at Edgar as though he were the intruder. Then they pushed past him into his shed. "'Ere!" shouted Edgar, "Get out of there!"

"Stay!" said Nova quietly as though to a stupid, but obedient, dog.

Edgar stayed. "Well, don't 'ee touch that compressor anyhow," he shouted.

The men emerged after a while, the pale blue man putting a small camera into his pocket. Bernard seemed pleased. He took Nova's hand and kissed it. "Ersss," he said. He waved vaguely at Edgar and the two men walked off towards a large black car parked down the road.

Nova called after them. "Au revoir Bernard," she said in a helpless little voice that Edgar didn't recognise, "Et merci bien!" Edgar put his arm round her but she shook him off.

Nova was quiet that evening. When Edgar went hopefully to bed she stayed up and in the morning she was gone. Edgar feared the worst, but she returned two days later smelling of train buffet miniatures. She steamrollered Edgar's quiet display of hurt feelings with enthusiasm. "Darling!" she said, "Such excitement. It's all arranged."

"What is?" asked Edgar. But she kissed him and they went to bed.

Edgar awoke the next morning to find Nova outside supervising

Fungus's car on to a low loader. "Where are you taking that?" he asked. She kissed him lightly. "To the gallery of course. Then we'll be back for the rest." Nova thrust a sheaf of papers into his hands.

The rest? As the truck drove away with the Vauxhall Nova Montage on its back, Edgar studied the paper. It was a contract for an exhibition. Nova had organised a one-man show at the Sunnyside Gallery. The contract was for a display of twenty "pieces" by her new discovery. Edgar.

He sat down hard on the kerb. Nova was again blurring the line between art and earning a living. How could he be an artist? He didn't have permission. But Nova assumed the right to give that permission and this seemed to be all that was necessary. Edgar was beginning to glimpse the mechanisms by which privilege is manifested.

Still, where was he to get "pieces"?

He placed an advert on the local commercial radio station. His offer of free motor makeovers was popular and soon every parking place in the street was occupied by a Cornish car tarnished by the salt winds of the west. They followed each other into his "studio" and over the next few days a Ford Sierra disguised as a wave, a Montego remade as a Wheelie Bin and a Fiat Punto disguised as a dog followed the Nova on to the lorry. He skilfully sprayed a Renault Espace into a preying mantis, a transit van became a balloon lifting into the sky and an ancient Mini Metro a lifeboat launching from Sennen Slip. A Vauxhall Astra was painted with stars, like a moonless night over water. A Jeep was steeped in blood, and bones crushed beneath its wheels. A Landrover became the blank face of incomprehension in heavily armed matt. Its cousin the Range Rover became an evocation of mislocated people living dislocated lives. A Mercedes became a dark-glassed symbol of light-fingered business. A BMW sucked in light.

Edgar's launch at the Sunnyside Gallery was the success of the season, and Nova the perfect hostess. Despite his prodigious work rate, there had not been time to paint the full complement of "pieces" so the "works" were augmented by gleaming showroom cars stolen to order by Shady Bunny Bennett. "Such irony!" noted a noted critic. "Ersss," opined Bernard, now revealed to be an arts potentate. There was a splendid catalogue and Nova's and Bernard's contacts ensured massive coverage in the national press.

Edgar had arrived.

But at night, lying next to Nova, he could not sleep. He had become the artist of Taking And Driving Away, the Sweeney Todd of car valeting. His street was a Bermuda Triangle of bangers. Led by the suntanned Fungus Rowe, the car owners' enquiries were becoming indignant and increasingly dangerous. This situation could not last.

Still, he lay next to Nova in her naked splendour, living in the present, waiting for the police to knock on his door.

For such is the life of the Cornish artist.

Gonamena Bedfellows

By Amanda Harris

"You look washed out, Tim. Are you not sleeping well?" "Not really," replied the boy, his head feeling like an overripe marrow. "Why not go back to bed?" "No...no way," he said more hastily than he'd intended. "I mean, I'd rather not."

For several nights now he had been wakened in the early hours by the feeling of someone getting into bed beside him; a hip bone rammed against his ribs, then a body curling up for sleep. Under the covers a strong smell of the earth, of deep caverns, a hint of metal and sweat. The first time it happened he switched on the light in terror, and scrambled out of bed to see what it was, but there was nothing, no one. Tentatively he got back under the duvet. The presence was still there. He clung to the side of the bed as if it were the last remnant of a sinking ship. The other body seemed to stretch and take up more of the space. Buoyed along through the darkness hours, Tim drifted in and out of sleep until, all of sudden, he felt the other body roll over, feet flat on the floor, and was gone. Light on – it was five o'clock. The bed warm where it had been. For five nights the routine had been exactly the same. Until last night, when a stink of stale tobacco and beery breath had snaked around the usual earth and sweat. Tim, who had sipped the odd shared glass of lager, had felt so sick he'd had to sit in the chair by the window, certain there was breathing under the bedclothes.

"And another thing, Tim", moaned his mother, "Why are your sheets so dirty these days – are you sleeping with your trainers on?" "Oh yes," said his father, "Your mother wants me to talk to you about smoking...you do know it isn't good for you, don't you?"

But Tim was asleep, head on the table, fingers lolling in his bowl of Rice Krispies.

They hadn't lived in the house for long. It had been a bargain as it needed modernising and house prices were lower in Cornwall than Gloucestershire. Before moving to Minions they had lived in a pretty village with a pond and a working pump, sheltered by mature oaks and Englishness. Lured to Cornwall by memories of childhood holidays and the distance from the M5, they had been dogged by a ferocious wind, an indefinable heritage from which they felt excluded and their inability to get anything finished; village greens replaced by moorland, games of cricket by standing stones

"Mr Arthur promised to be here this morning to plumb in the bath," complained the mother. "I haven't seen the builder all week and then the man with the carpets arrived yesterday and there are no floors to put them on. The cupboards are full of mildew, and I don't know how we're going to fit in all our furniture. And have you seen that rusty metal and old machinery in the field down the lane. And why don't they put latches on their gates? Every single one is tied up with string!"

Rough pasture, denuded trees, relentless rain. It felt like an alien world.

By the fifth night Tim knew what to expect. He wasn't comfortable sharing his bed with a stranger but began to relax a little into the routine that didn't vary; the presence was never restless, seemed to fall into an immediate sleep and then would be gone by dawn.

Daytimes he began to explore the neighbourhood. The first time when walking down the footpath towards the South Caradon Mine, he'd had the overwhelming feeling of literally "swimming against the tide". He was alone but he felt buffeted against a crowd walking determinedly up the hill, that same smell of earth and sweat. He looked around to see if there was anyone else nearby and was nearly knocked over by the force of the throng. And then they were gone.

After school he rushed down the old tramline with his new friends Sally and Max Kittow. Together they crawled up adits, dropped stones and the remains of their packed lunches down mine shafts, peering over the edge into the deep darkness. They slid down the old scree slopes, told jokes in the engine houses and kicked lazily at the rabbit droppings. Tim found it hard to keep up with the two children as they scuttled over the rough terrain like mountain goats.

"Let's go over Phoenix…you seen that hole over Glasgow…let's go!"

They dashed ahead, clashing shoulders and shrieking in a scuffle to avoid the puddles. All of a sudden, Tim was once again beaten back by a determined force marching against him. He tripped on a rock and fell backwards into the muddy track. Huge boots tramped by his head, sending up storms of sodden earth and ringing granite. He shouted out to his friends but they were gone. Why had they not been stopped?

He pulled himself up on to a protruding rock and stared out over the landscape formed and shaped by a lust for minerals. What was going on? He was completely confused.

"Awright there boy? Look like you seen a ghost. You the boy from up Gonamena?"

Tim nodded. An old man leaning on two sticks looked up at him.

"I heard there was new people in. Like it? 'Ansome 'ouse that one. I had a great-uncle lived there afore he went South Dakota. It was a hostel for the miners in them days. There was loads of 'em lived in there. They would hot bed with someone on another shift – day shift would leave at 5am, bed warmed up for the night shift boys. How many of you live up there now?"

"Well there's Mum and Dad and my two sisters and me – five."

"Five! There'd 've been 50 of them when they was mining South Caradon. And what makes me sad, boy, is that you'd never know now that all they men were working this land, night and day, extracting its riches, it's all so quiet. Just a few old 'uns shuffling about, heads crammed with memories, hands hard from grappling with rock."

It was Spring 1880. Moses Togwell, sat on his bed, the one he shared with Arthur May – Arthur did nights and he did days, so they shared the bed and halved the rent. He was counting his money, as he did most weeks. Two guineas more and he'd have his passage to America, to South Dakota where he'd heard there were riches untold. Six more months he reckoned and he'd have enough – after his bed rent and deductions to the mine for food and barbering plus the bit he'd send back to his mother and sisters in St Just. He'd worked down Botallack for five years but when that was closed down he'd come up to Minions where South Caradon was the richest copper mine in the area. Loads of them had moved up to Bodmin Moor; not much chance for fishing up here. It was a mad place; full of men with nothing to do but work, drink and pray. Some of them had built their own houses or shacks but they weren't homely, no one wanted to stay in them. Saturday nights were the worst, Saturday pay day even more so – the beer flowed like lava and ignited the veins of the displaced miners; mole-like by day, minotaur by night.

"Have you seen this article in the Cornish Times? About a Mrs

Martin?" Tim's mother had been about to scan the small ads trying to find an electrician who could fix the wiring which seemed to fuse each time they turned on the bathroom light, when her eye had alighted on the story. She began to read. "Mrs Martin, mother of Kylie aged six and baby David, had been hanging out her washing last Wednesday when she began to feel the earth slip from under her feet. "I thought it was an earthquake and then suddenly this huge crack appeared in my garden. I jumped to one side just in time as an enormous hole opened up and my washing basket, with Kylie's brand new school uniform in it, disappeared. I screamed. Suddenly, the slide and sandpit went down too. Luckily I grabbed David's pram and we ran out into the road – I was worried about the cat but I found her sleeping in the airing cupboard. It was a terrifying experience".

Robert Dounsey, the conservation officer from Caradon District Council told the Cornish Times: "Underneath Minions is a maze of tunnels and caverns, more complex than a map of the London Underground and the roofs of the tunnels are very close to the surface in many cases. These incidents are quite rare but obviously very frightening when they do occur."

"What is it with this place? How can people have left it like this? Why didn't they fill in the tunnels? How could they have left these dangerous holes for future generations? That poor woman – what if her baby had gone down too? What would that man from the district council have said then… 'We deeply regret…the price of history'."

"Mine Cap'n wants to see us." The word was passed back down the line as the night shift climbed wearily towards the daylight. They hung up their lamps and all shuffled out into the bright sunlight. It was July and the swallows were swooping low. Moses stretched his back, conscious of the weight of his savings in the inner lining of his waistcoat. He was nearly there – two months more perhaps. But the rumour was that the price of copper was falling so low that. No one wanted to consider what might happen. The mine captain was a stout man with a nose for minerals. He knew how to exploit a lode, to send it to grass, to encourage his men to dig deeper and further. His life was his mine, the South Caradon mine. He had seen it thrive and become the third largest copper producing mine in the West of England. Steam, power, teams of men all harnessed to the cause of bringing the "flashing diamond into light". He was not a man of poetry

but he loved those lines by John Harris —

Yoking the elements in brotherhood
To belch the flashing diamond into light
And vomit forth the backbone of the world

*They seemed to encompass his world. His world that was about to change
for ever. The copper standard was now so low that the mine owners were
considering closure. Lay-offs at first and then winding up. The men, black
faced, assembled round him.*

*The Cornish Times 1880. It was announced today that the South Caradon
Mine is to close. Five hundred men will be laid off in the next two months
and a further two hundred by the end of the year. The men listened in
shocked silence as they were informed by the Mine Captain, Mr John
Holman, a lay preacher.*

It was Sunday afternoon and Tim was mooching about on Craddock
Moor vaguely wondering how he was going to explain another pair of ripped
and shredded jeans. He thought he heard hammering and clambered over a
mound to find out who or what it was. The hammering got louder, metal
against rock. Then all went quiet. All of a sudden a huge booming sound; an
explosion. Tim leapt back instinctively but nothing moved except the daisies
in the breeze. It was coming from underground. The hammering started up
again and heavy machinery was cranked and turned. From out of the metallic
cacophony other sounds emerged.

*Copper...Cuprite...Tenorite...Malachite...Azurite...Chalcocite...Copper
...Cuprite...Tenorite...Malachite...Azurite...Chalcocite...Copper...*

Tim sat and listened – something was going on underground. From
nowhere Sally and Max appeared. He told them about the explosion and the
hammering. "We gotta dig," they shouted. They ran back to Gonamena and
grabbed a spade and pick from the garden shed. Down the bottom of the
garden behind the apple tree, Tim began to excavate. Sally and Max took
their turn. At first the earth, well watered, was soft and giving. But soon they
reached rock and the pick end broke. They used their hands, they devised
levers.

"What is going on out there?" his father called "Just looking Dad, it's
fine." At night they covered the hole with a tarpaulin.

The next day they were back with renewed vigour. By afternoon they had struck a wooden beam and his father took a shift as curiosity got the better of him. His mother, sceptical at first, got on her knees and began scraping inside the hole with a trowel.

The wood gave way to a void. Tim flashed his torch into the darkness which glinted back at him. "I'm going down!" he said. They lowered the builder's ladder. Tim slowly and solemnly descended into the pit. The others waited in tense silence. "Eureka!" he shouted, re-emerging, "We've struck copper! We've struck copper!"

Moses Togwell, tears in his eyes, turns his back on Cornwall. The wind off the Atlantic is brisk as he faces the New World and the Black Hills of South Dakota.

Annie Pascoe's Man

by Pauline Sheppard

It's true, I saw him with my own eyes. I can see him now, exactly as though I was standin' there lookin' at him for the first time, Annie Pascoe's Man. Caused a stir I can tell you, everyone was talkin' about it. Well, they would, wouldn't they? You can't keep a thing like that quiet, not in a small village.

Mind, Annie always was different. Dozy Annie we used to call her on account of she was always one step behind. Part of the gang and outside it all to once, moonin' around an starin' out to sea, spent hours starin' at the sea. She could be all there when she wanted to be, but that wasn't very often. Never drank or smoked much but Will Thomas give her a reefer the night she went off on the back of Ben Pascoe's BSA Bantam; Ben bought a mini a few months later, on account of Annie an' the baby.

There was a whole rash of weddings 'bout then, some survive an' some don't. Annie an' Ben survived, Ben didn't seem to mind Annie wanderin' off so to speak, he got used to burnt toast.

Still, whatever it seem like on the surface, you don't know what's on underneath, you never know what's really goin' on, the undercurrent. You can live right next door to someone for years, know their favourite telly programme, what they like for tea, hear the water runnin' bathtime, know what time they come in an' go out and not know them at all. That's how it was with Annie Pascoe's man. Friday afternoon art class, that's when it started. No good would come of it, we all said that. They was all incomers an' hippies went there, an' anyway what about Ben? What'd Ben have to say?

"Nothin'." said Annie. "He doesn't know."

Well, he soon did, can't keep a thing like that from your husband, can you?

Ellie Trahair at the shop found out first when Annie changed her regular shopping time to Friday mornings instead of afternoons. Ellie put two and two together because she'd seen Annie take one of those adult education leaflets from the Post Office section. *Expanding Horizons* it's called. She and Lizzie James were talking about it when Mrs Jenkin came in with Danny – he's the simple one who's on the government training scheme on the *Jenny Lowe*, Ben's boat.

"That Annie Pascoe think she's a cut above the rest of us," says Lizzie.

"Well," said Mrs Jenkin, "Let's look up in the leaflet an' see what 'tis she's doin'."

"It's Art!" said Ellie. "Beginners Art Classes at the Old Sail Loft."

"Painting an' that?"

"Whatever do she want to do that for?"

"Men with no clothes on!"

"Lizzie James!"

Mrs Jenkin nodded in Danny's direction but he was keeping quiet over by the frozen foods. Danny has a way of being there without being there, if you know what I mean.

Well, Danny told Mitch an' Mitch told his dad, Will Morris. Will's skipper of the *Jenny Lowe*, an' Will told Ben.

"Wouldn't let my wife mix with they up country folk."

But Ben wasn't like that. Might have been better if he had put his foot down, tried to stop it there and then but Ben, well he just laughed.

"Let her go 'head," he said. "What harm can it do? 'Tis a fad s'all."

"Might be right, Ben, might be." Will Morris d'know a thing or two about people. "Kids grown up now aren't they?"

"Ess. Roy's livin' over to Penzance an' Jean's up country working."

"Time on her hands see, time on her hands."

"Least I know where she's to."

Did he though? I mean she was there in body, but in mind? Well, it's like I said to Lizzie, Annie was always somewhere else. 'Tis a dangerous thing, go out too far an' you might not come back, plenty like that up Bodmin. She always had a bit of a thing about the artists – used to watch them out on the beach. Funny lot, all over paint an' holes, not a smart one amongst them. In the old days it was all fish, all along the front here, cellars and lofts; hard work an' heavy for man and woman alike. Nowadays there's more artists than fishermen in the lofts, specially since the Art School opened. Studios all along. Queer things they paint too, not pictures, well, not what I'd call a picture, a tree's a tree not a big red splodge. I agree with Ben on that.

Annie only ever brought one picture home, pleased as punch she was when she showed us in the shop. We didn't say nothin'. Well, it's like when the kids bring pictures home from school, what can you say? Stick it on the fridge for a few days 'til they've forgotten about it, then pound of potatoes, cabbage, pint of milk – what else you gonna do with it?

It might have been different if she'd chosen another subject but it was the *Jenny Lowe* – you could tell that by the name, and the colour – the colour was right on the boat anyhow.

"It's all wrong!" Ben was horrified. "She'd sink if the wheelhouse was up forward like that!"

"Peter said it was best in the class."

"Who's Peter?"

"Teacher."

"He d'know no more about art than he do about fishing boats."

"'Tis expression."

"What of?"

"Feelin'."

"Said you'd be home by four."

"I had to finish the painting."

"Why couldn't you finish it next time?"

"The light. Morning light isn't the same as evening light an' the light tomorrow mightn't be the same as the light today."

Well, as Ben said, that was a sayin' to beat all, specially as the sky behind the *Jenny Lowe* was bright green. Whoever'd seen a bright green sky?

"Peter showed me. It happens just before the sun sets – a flash of green."

Like Ben said, there's snooker table green an' sky green an' that sky was snooker table green.

That was the first and last time Annie brought a picture home.

Things went on as usual for a bit. Will an' Mitch an' the rest'd razz Ben up by alluding to "Life Classes" an' the like but that didn't last long. There were more important things to talk about like the latest fish quota and the draw for the euchre tournament.

Then Annie started to go to Friday evening class as well as the afternoon one. Nothin' changed on the surface, Ben's supper was always ready, even if she had to prepare it the night before. Annie discovered the power of order. Sometimes she'd leave a note next to the oven gloves, if it was a casserole. There were a lot of notes. They didn't often have Friday supper together. They didn't often do much together at all. Annie was always off painting.

In fact there wasn't an afternoon went by she didn't just pop into the shop on the way to the Art School.

"You got another lesson, Annie?"

"Peter's helpin' me with perspective."

"What's that then?"

"Oh, you know, distance between things."

"Oh 'ess."

Then it was composition needed some attention, or colour. People were beginning to talk. Mrs Jenkin told Lizzie she'd seen Annie walking the cliff path with her so-called teacher.

"Him with the ponytail."

"Got a ring in his eyebrow?"

"That's Annie Pascoe's man."

Ben was like a fish out of water. Home was his safe harbour an' Annie was his anchor. He didn't always go out of an evening, fact was he didn't go out as much as some of the others. Sometimes he'd bring her some Guinness, Annie was partial to a glass of Guinness, and they'd sit an' watch television together. They were Ben's happiest moments, all cosy an' safe with Annie sittin' across the fire from him. He knew there was another world behind her eyes and he'd got used to replacing kettle elements, scraping burned toast and finding lost keys. In fact it made him feel right, it was something he could touch. If he hadn't had that he might lose contact an' she'd drift off. It was a rhythm as predictable as the tide, it could be stormy with a crash of ten broken tea cups or lap in gentle with laughter like when she put a jumper on back to front. It was charted water, but now, just when life should be settlin' down, children all growed up, time for Ben and Annie to enjoy each other's company, here was everything all topsy turvy, flotsam and jetsam, he was adrift, more often than not coming home to an empty house, a strangely ordered and unfamiliar place, a foreign shore. Ben was used to tacking round spilled boxes, dirty dishes and abandoned hoovers. He didn't like these unfamiliar waters.

"You spend a lot of time at that Art School."

"Where's the harm?"

"It's not like you."

"Isn't it?"

Well, as I said to Lizzie, I never saw anyone look so bereft as Ben Pascoe, an' what about the other? Why didn't he ask about the young man with the ponytail?

Things came to a head, usually do. November seventh it was. The *Jenny Lowe* ran aground in rough seas off Spain; got back all right but had to put up for repairs so the crew found themselves home for a while.

Danny spent a lot of time round Ben's. He was there when Annie unpacked her shopping basket, just a few things she'd got on the way back from Friday afternoon class: potatoes, broccoli, teabags and a new tube of Titanium White.

"My Christ Almighty I could buy enough emulsion to do the whole kitchen for that price!"

"Doesn't go far," said Annie. "There's a sale on at the Art Shop, might get some brushes tomorrow."

"We can't afford it! Clive down the yard says it could be a month before we put out. It was bad enough already with the quotas an' all. With me at home there's no money coming in. How much are these art classes anyway?"

"I pay for Friday afternoon that's all. The other times Peter gives me free tuition."

"You spend a lot of time with that Peter!" It was out, he'd said it, and Danny was his witness.

"It's the exhibition."

"What exhibition?"

"At the end of the course."

"End of the course?"

"In three weeks time. I don't know what I'll do with myself when it's over."

"You'll find something, maid, don't worry." Ben was happy again; just so long as he knew when the end was, when his Annie would come back to him, sit across the fire of an evening watching television instead of painting lop-sided boats and green skies. He was so happy he took Danny for a drink, dry land was in sight.

The Invitation to the opening was propped up in front of their wedding photograph on the mantelpiece for two weeks. Ben saw it every time he went into the sitting room.

You are cordially invited to the opening of
Pride of Place
an exhibition of new work by local artists
to be held at the Art School
Friday 4th December
7.30-9 pm

"You don't want me there," he'd said.

"How not?"

"Wouldn't fit in."

"Don't know 'til you try."

There was another invitation in the pub.

"I been to one of they," said Will Morris, "lot of people standing round with wine an' pontificating is all it is. Still, always come down the pub after."

And a poster in the shop.

As Lizzie said, "Won't all be hippies an' artists 'cos all Annie's friends will be there, so it isn't as though we won't know anyone."

The big fish loft was packed to the gunnels. We was all there – me, Lizzie, Mrs Jenkin, Ellie Trahair, Mitch and Will Morris, Danny, all the crew. Big gathering it was.

Beneath the swell of pontification, strong currents ran in the fishloft, and a storm raged in Ben Pascoe. Ellie said his knuckles were white even before he come up the stairs.

In the morning Annie was back home, sitting across the fire from Ben. Familiar waters, yet nothin' was the same, like the refit on the *Jenny Lowe*, same wheelhouse, same bows, same trawl, everythin' look the same as before but everythin' feel different.

How did she know? She hadn't seen the sea boil and rage over the stern, she hadn't seen a man lose his hand in the winching gear. How could she see that? How could this painter of snooker-table green skies see into a man's soul? It was him and somehow not him at all and more than him all to once. It showed a part of him even he was afraid to see. Naked, those eyes were naked, hiding nothing.

The picture hung between them. *The Fisherman* by Annie Pascoe. Ben looked across at his wife. Annie's eyes smiled back, but she was staring through and beyond him, she had the horizon in her sights.

He recognised Annie Pascoe's Man but as for its creator, Ben realised he didn't know her at all.

Doubtful Island

By Mercedes Kemp

*Until we know considerably more about the geography of our planet than we do
now, there will always be 'doubtful islands', distinguished on the Admiralty charts
by the sceptical affix 'E.D.' (existence doubtful) or 'P.D.' (position doubtful).*
With grateful thanks to Lieut-Commander Rupert T Gould, R N

My name is Angelina, although not my real name, which cannot be
spoken. Sometimes I dream that I can undo my steps, that afternoon
follows night and morning afternoon and then it is night again, that the wind
does not blow our sails on to this land of strangers, but sucks us back home,
to the only ground my feet can tread without hurting.

We were brought here by force, and by force we were made to do
that which we do best, turning our love of work into hard labour. We came
from a land of proud washerwomen, mistresses of wind and water, suds and
starch. Our elders had been taught the art by the veiled women of Larochel.
As children we were initiated into the secrets of organdie and muslin, batiste,
percale, holland and dimity; if we showed real promise we were sent to the
great washing-hall where Madame Blanchisseuse, who had herself been
taught at the mythic Larochel, would instruct us on the higher art of
laundering ninon, pongee, tussore, fustian and guipure. So deep was our love
of well tended cloth that the flight of a woman's underskirts was known to
ensnare men's hearts and send them baying at the moon like love-sick dogs.
We loved nothing better than the sight, sound and scent of our great washing
lines dancing and shimmering against the summer sky.

It was on one such morning that the ships arrived. By nightfall the
houses were burned, the great washing-hall razed to the ground and the
newly washed sheets rent and trodden into the dirt. The boarding of the ships
I do not wish to remember, nor the journey which cast us asunder, each ship
bound for a different destination. Madame Blanchisseuse could not be found,
and now we must do without her. This is hard, for she was our memory and
our imagination, she reminded us of who we are and what we have done.

And now, here we are, washed up on this land where wind and water
do not seem to know their place, clinging together more than would appear
seemly, forming the damp, turbulent fog that turns the freshly laundered

cloths (not our cloths, but still the carriers of our art) into heavy, mould-ridden, dank-smelling foul things that injure our sensibilities. And yet we hope, as only landless people can, and we dream of home each night. Come soon. Come soon.

This morning, out on the horizon, there is a pink sliver of light we have not seen before. It is the colour and texture of organdie and it billows against the grey sky like a great sail made of finely woven light. We wash no more, transfixed by this vision, which seems to get closer to the river mouth, and more distinct, appearing and disappearing as if following the buoys which signal the channel to the harbour. Closer and closer it comes, until we can see that this dome of different sky has different birds flying within it, and land beneath, floating along towards the Carrick Roads, propelled by the swelling of row upon row of such beautifully laundered washing lines as would make one's heart swell with pleasure. And on the highest line of all, nine white cloths, all in the shape of lateen sails, bear the inscription ANARCADIA, and we know in our hearts that this is our land come to fetch us and that there, amongst the washing, Madame Blanchisseuse is fussing with her oeuvre, smoothing a ruffle here, tweaking a stubborn hem and a frisky flounce there, for the washing must be perfection when her children finally come home.

For the Acadian people of the Canadian Eastern seaboard who, in 1757, were expelled from their settlements and placed in a prisoner of war camp at Penryn.